Let's Look at Beans

Katie Peters

GRL Consultants,
Diane Craig and Monica Marx,
Certified Literacy Specialists

Pull Ahead Readers

Lerner Publications ◆ Minneapolis

Note from a GRL Consultant
This Pull Ahead leveled book has been carefully designed for beginning readers. A team of guided reading literacy experts has reviewed and leveled the book to ensure readers pull ahead and experience success.

Lerner Publications Company
An imprint of Lerner Publishing Group, Inc.
241 First Avenue North
Minneapolis, MN 55401 USA

For reading levels and more information, look up this title at www.lernerbooks.com.

Main body text set in Memphis Pro 24/39
Typeface provided by Linotype.

Photo Acknowledgments
The images in this book are used with the permission of: © arkady2013/iStockphoto, pp. 12, 13; © caoyu36/iStockphoto, pp. 10, 11, 16 (bean pods); © Christian Meyer Design/iStockphoto, pp. 4, 5, 16 (bean seeds); © flisak/iStockphoto, p. 3; © martinturzak/iStockphoto, pp. 14, 15; © weisschr/iStockphoto, pp. 8, 9, 16 (flowers); © wuviveka/iStockphoto, pp. 6, 7, 16 (plants).

Front cover: © wuviveka/iStockphoto

Library of Congress Cataloging-in-Publication Data

Names: Peters, Katie, author.
Title: Let's look at beans / Katie Peters.
Description: Minneapolis : Lerner Publications, [2021] | Series: Plant life cycles (pull ahead readers - nonfiction) | Includes index. | Audience: Ages 4–7 | Audience: Grades K–1 | Summary: "Introduce emergent readers to the life cycle of the mighty bean. Carefully leveled text and bright photos show bean plants in all their stages: seed, sprout, flower, pod. Pairs with the fiction title Bean Soup."— Provided by publisher.
Identifiers: LCCN 2019045810 (print) | LCCN 2019045811 (ebook) | ISBN 9781541590243 (library binding) | ISBN 9781728403120 (paperback) | ISBN 9781728400747 (ebook)
Subjects: LCSH: Beans—Life cycles—Juvenile literature.
Classification: LCC SB327 .P425 2021 (print) | LCC SB327 (ebook) | DDC 635/.65—dc23

LC record available at https://lccn.loc.gov/2019045810
LC ebook record available at https://lccn.loc.gov/2019045811

Manufactured in the United States of America
4-1011199-48078-1/13/2025

Contents

Let's Look at Beans

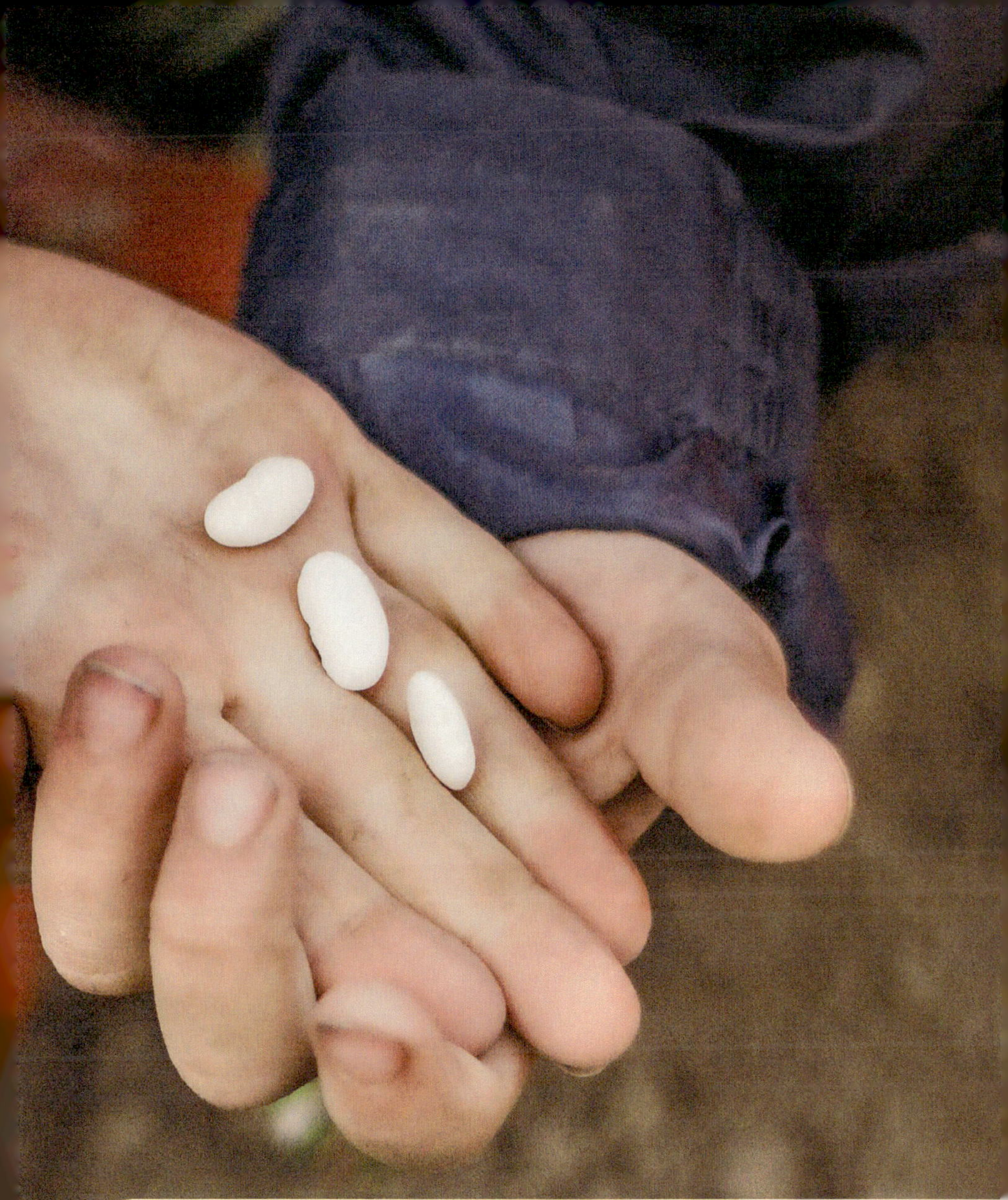

See the bean seeds.

See the bean plants.

See the bean flowers.

See the bean pods.

We pick the beans.

We cook the beans.

Did You See It?

bean flowers

bean plants

bean pods

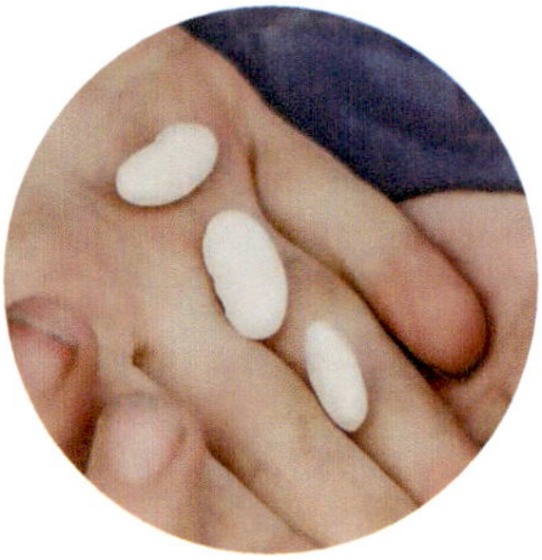
bean seeds

Index